BOOK #2

OTTO UNDERCOVER

★ CANYON CATASTROPHE ★

RHEA PERLMAN

ILLUSTRATED BY

DAN SANTAT

KATHERINE TEGEN BOOKS

An Imprint of HarperCollinsPublishers

For my mom and dad,
And for Bandy Venditti
and the Banes

Otto Undercover #2: Canyon Catastrophe

Text copyright © 2006 by Rhea Perlman

Illustrations copyright © 2006 by Dan Santat

Library of Congress Cataloging-in-Publication Data

Perlman, Rhea.

   Canyon catastrophe / Rhea Perlman ; illustrated by Dan Santat.— 1st ed.

     p. cm. — (Otto undercover; #2)

   Summary: With the help of his aunts and his trusty racecar, undercover agent Otto Pillip sets out to stop a criminal from blowing up the Grand Canyon. Includes words spelled backward, anagrams, and palindromes.

   ISBN-10: 0-06-075498-2 (trade ed.) — ISBN-13: 978-0-06-075498-3 (trade ed.)

   ISBN-10: 0-06-075497-4 (pbk. ed.) — ISBN-13: 978-0-06-075497-6 (pbk. ed.)

   [1. Spies—Fiction. 2. Aunts—Fiction. 3. Automobiles, Racing—Fiction. 4. Grand Canyon (Ariz.)—Fiction. 5. Word games—Fiction. 6. Humorous stories.] I. Santat, Dan, ill. II. Title.

PZ7.P43243Can 2006   2005006215

[Fic]—dc22   CIP

                                                                                                          AC

1 2 3 4 5 6 7 8 9 10
❖
First Edition

CONTENTS

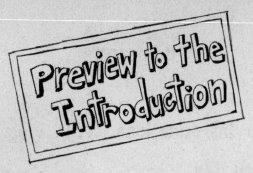

Stuff You Can Skip

If you read Book One, you can skip the chapters called The Other Preview to the Introduction and The Introduction, because you know that stuff already.

Or you might want to read them anyway, in case some parts are funny.

Another suggestion is to use your spare time doing something useful, like picking your toenails or putting your hand in your armpit and making some terrific farting noises.

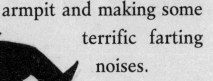

Word Puzzle Alert!!!

Look out for backward words!!

Retirw is backward for *writer*.

Watch out for anagrams!! Anagrams are words that become other words when their letters are all scrambled up.

Sword is an anagram for *words*, and *red ear* is an anagram for *reader*.

Keep your *eye* out for palindromes, which are words that are spelled exactly the same backward and forward, like *boob*.

If you think the *retirw* is a **boob** for making the ***red ears*** waste their time figuring out word puzzles all day long, don't worry, you don't actually have to do them.

The answers are on the sides of the pages.

Otto Asks a Question

"Hey, you want to hear this song?" asked Otto.

"No," said everyone.

He sang it anyway.

The Song Otto Sang

Otto, By Otto
(In the note of G)

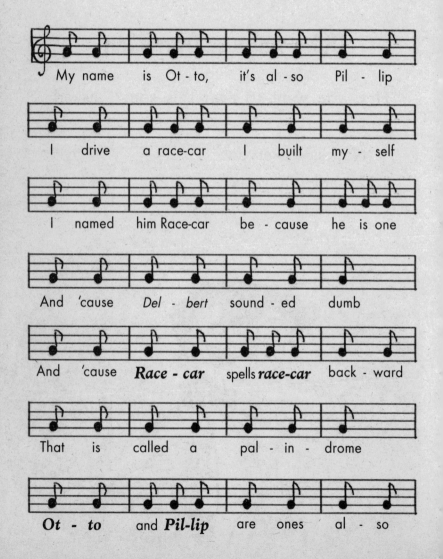

CHAPTER 1/3

How Are Things?

Not good.

About 500 miles away, a large little girl was skipping into a famous national park. She was carrying a Weewee the Pup tent and 10,000 sticks of dynamite.

CHAPTER 1

Road Trip

At the very same moment, Otto's Aunt FooFoo was backing an ice-cream truck out of the garage. Aunt FiFi was next to her in the passenger seat, and Otto was passed out in the back. It was the first time he had slept in a week. He had gotten a letter from his parents that said he should keep his *eye* out for signs of his first mission as a secret agent, and he had been afraid to close it and miss something.

As FooFoo pulled onto the highway, FiFi broke the silence with her vocal exercises, which consisted of shrieking the

Eye is a palindrome.

note of A-flat over and over. It was the only note she knew.

Otto sprang up, smashing his head on the roof of the truck. His heart was pumping, his *eye* was oozing, and his head hurt like crazy.

"Did I miss anything?" asked Otto, sitting straight up in the backseat.

"Only all of August and half of September," said FiFi.

"What?!" said Otto.

"She's kidding," said FooFoo. "Aren't you?"

"Beats me," said FiFi.

Otto checked his watch. No days had passed. He'd been asleep for 6¼ hours.

"Where are we going?" asked Otto.

"We're taking you to the beach, Ottie. Your mind is mush, and you need a vacation," said Aunt FooFoo.

Suddenly Otto was fully awake.

"Stop the car!" he screamed. "I'm calling a meeting."

CHAPTER 2

A Meeting

"Okay, the meeting is called to order." Otto raised his hand. "I call on myself."

"That figures," said FiFi.

"First of all, there is no relaxing in the secret agent business. *Action* is *a tonic*."

"Blah blah blah," said FooFoo.

"Millionth of all, we're supposed to be undercover. Remember?!"

There was a good possibility they remembered. The Aunts had spent the whole week assisting Otto in developing a material to act as a disguise for Racecar in order to protect his identity.

The material was a jellylike substance that could form into the shape of any vehicle that Otto had designed on his

Action is an anagram for a tonic.

15

computer. At the moment, it was hardened into the shape of an ice-cream truck.

"My parents said that I'm the only one who doesn't need a disguise, because most adults and all bad guys can't tell one kid from the other," said Otto. "But where are your disguises?"

"Whoops, I knew we forgot something," said FooFoo.

"Oh noooo," said Otto.

"I guess we're going to have to use these," said FiFi.

She opened the glove compartment and took out two wigs, two mustaches, and one beard. She and FooFoo put them on.

They were disguised as The Uncles, FroFro and FriFri.

"Got ya!" said FroFro.

This Is Confusing

All these names may seem confusing, but they're really not. See, Aunt FooFoo was Uncle FroFro, and Aunt FiFi was Uncle FriFri, but Otto, who always called his aunts by their backward names, Aunt *OofOof* and Aunt *IfIf*, also called his uncles by their backward names, Uncle *OrfOrf* and Uncle *IrfIrf*. In front of other people, FooFoo called FiFi FriFri, and FriFri called FooFoo FroFro. Except when they forgot and called each other FiFi and FooFoo.

Glad we straightened that out.

CHAPTER 3 1/4

A Question

Okay, but what about the little girl with the 10,000 sticks of dynamite and the Weewee the Pup tent?

An Answer

She's up to no good.

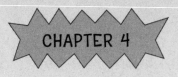

CHAPTER 4

Knock Knock

There was a knock on the door of the truck. They looked out the window and saw a line of kids outside waiting for ice cream.

"Oh no, they think we really have ice cream," said Otto.

"Did you bring any ice cream?" FooFoo asked FiFi.

"No, I didn't bring any ice cream. Did you bring any ice cream?" she asked FooFoo.

"I didn't bring any ice cream," said FooFoo. "Did you bring any, Ottie?"

"I didn't even know I was coming," said Otto.

"Don't worry, I'll take care of it," said FooFoo.

FroFro, who was FooFoo, lowered the window.

"What are your flavors, please?" asked the first customer.

"Tell them we're closed!" whispered Otto desperately.

FroFro took a deep breath. "We have

chocolate caramel perky peanut butter crunch, banana bubblegum cookie-dough-re-mi, cheesecake sweet cream eggnog crazy cashew, and nonfat piña colada, all homemade, nice."

"We do?" said Otto.

"Made 'em fresh this morning," said FooFoo, who was one of the world's best cooks.

"Got ya again!" said FiFi.

Both aunts thought this was a riot, even FiFi, who had only laughed about six times before in her life. They doubled over in hysterics.

CHAPTER 5

A Sign

They were back on the road, after scooping out ice cream to 29 kids. Otto was in the passenger seat, but he was the one actually controlling the car. FiFi just made believe she was driving.

Otto was on his fourth ice-cream cone. He was probably the only kid in the world who liked the cone better than the ice cream. He had invented the double cone-cone, which was an ice-cream cone with a scoop of ice cream in it with another cone on top.

"I'm 100 percent against this beach thing," said Otto. "I hate water and I can't swim."

"I brought your dolphin water

wings," said Aunt FooFoo.

Otto was way too old for his dolphin water wings.

"I'm not going." He was about to turn the truck around when he noticed a sign up ahead on the highway. It said:

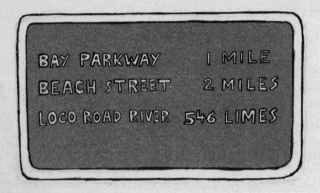

BAY PARKWAY   1 MILE
BEACH STREET   2 MILES
LOCO ROAD RIVER 546 LIMES

Otto's heart started beating fast.

"Did you see that sign?" he asked excitedly.

"Yes, we're almost there!" said FooFoo, putting big globs of sunblock all over her body.

"I think that some of the words in that sign are anagrams," said Otto, already

rearranging the letters in his head.

"Oh, what fun," said FooFoo, "that the highway people put a puzzle on the road. Fi, get out a pad and a pencil."

"I don't want to," said FiFi.

"Never mind, I figured it out!" said Otto. A big smile came over his face. "I'm glad we have a lot of ice cream, because 546 miles is a long way."

"Yes, it is," said FiFi. "It's a good thing we're only going two miles to Beach Street."

"Change of plans," said Otto. "That sign was a sign. We just got our first communication. We're going to the Colorado River!"

Canyon Catastrophe

PART TWO
EVEN THOUGH THERE WASN'T A PART ONE

Exactly 546 miles and $\frac{1}{4}$ of a page later, they pulled off the road and into the parking lot of the Colorado River Bait and Tackle Shop. It was just opening up.

27

CHAPTER 6

Bob

There was a man at the counter.

"Do you have a ladies' room?" asked FooFoo, immediately forgetting that she was supposed to be a guy.

Otto pinched his aunt.

"Ouch," she said.

"Yes sir, we do ditty do have one," said the man. "Is there a lady with you?"

"Oh, uh, no," said FooFoo, realizing she shouldn't have asked for the ladies' room. "I was just checking in case a lady came in while I was here. Then, if you were busy doing things, I could point it out to her, and she wouldn't get cranky waiting for you. You know those ladies—they can get pretty cranky. Do you have a men's room?"

28

"In the back," said the man.

FiFi went up to the counter.

"I'd like a pole and bait for catching whatever you've got in this river," she said in the deepest voice she could.

"Have you ever fished before?" asked the man.

"Of course I've fished before," said FiFi, who was easily insulted. "I've fished in

all the mighty waters of the United States and Zanzibar. I've caught leaf fish, needlefish, cigar shark, freshwater batfish, and Alabama hogsucker, to name a few."

"We mostly have trout here," he said.

"Oh, well, I've never caught any of those," said FiFi.

"That's okey-dokey day," said the man. "I'll get you everything you're going to need. And would you like a rod too, sir?" he asked FooFoo, who had returned from the men's room.

"Who are you calling *sir*?" she said, forgetting again that she was disguised as a man.

"That's all right," said Otto. "My uncle doesn't need a rod. He's a cook. But I'll take one, please."

"All righty rooty, son. I'll be just a minute."

He ducked down under the counter and

came up with a big box of fishing supplies.

"That was pretty speedy of you, sir," said Otto.

"You can call me *Bob*," said the man.

Otto looked at the name tag on the man's shirt.

"The tag on your shirt says your name's Clyde," said Otto.

"That's right," said the man, "but you can call me *Bob*."

Otto actually loved the name *Bob* because it is a palindrome.

"Okay then, *Bob*, how much do we owe you?" asked Otto.

"That'll be $87.78. Have fun *farting* through the Grand *Noynac*."

"Sir!" said FooFoo, forgetting once more about her disguise, "there are ladies present."

31

The message hit Otto like a ton of bricks. He had just gotten his next communication. He was thinking that he needed a pencil and paper to figure this one out.

"Perhaps you'd like a pencil and paper," said **Bob** mysteriously.

"Yes, thank you," said Otto.

While his "Uncles" were paying for the supplies, Otto went to a corner of the store and tried to work out the message.

"If I rearrange the letters in *farting*, I get, um, *ant frig*," he said to himself. "No, that's not it. Let's see," he said, trying again, "how about *nag rift*? No, not that either." He sighed. "Is it *fat grin*? No, no. Wait a minute, wait a minute, it's coming," he said, getting very excited. "Aha! *Farting* is *rafting*. Have fun rafting through the Grand *Noynac*."

He saw the rest immediately. *Noynac* was backward for *Canyon*. That made total sense. The Colorado River goes right through the Grand Canyon.

"We'd like to buy a raft, please, and five life jackets," he yelled over to *Bob*. Otto needed the extra life jackets because he couldn't swim.

"All righty rooty, son," said *Bob*.

Otto hadn't seen his parents since he was two, and had no memory of what they

looked like. He had to be sure. He asked
Bob, "Are you my *dad*?"

"Is your name John Knickerbocker?"
asked **Bob**.

"No," said Otto.

"Guess not, then," said **Bob**.

"Oh," said Otto.

He figured there were other
secret operatives in the agency
besides his parents and
himself. Secretly he
was glad that his dad
wasn't the kind
of person who said
goofy things like
"all righty rooty"
and "okey-dokey
day."

"If you're all
finished now, fellas,
I'll be closing up the

store," said **Bob**, pushing them out the door.

"But you just opened up," said Otto.

"Yup, short day," said **Bob**.

"Who do you think you're calling *fellas*?" said FooFoo as they walked out of the store.

CHAPTER 7

Some Holes

"Uncle **OrfOrf**, please slow down," said Otto.

FooFoo, who did everything fast, was rowing the raft like she was competing for a gold medal. Otto hated rivers just as much as he hated oceans. He was wearing three life jackets.

"Uncle **IrfIrf**, please sit down. You're rocking the boat," he said.

FiFi was standing up in the raft, fishing. She was so tiny that every time they went through a rough part of the river, she fell overboard. FiFi could swim, but that counted as exercise, and FiFi refused to exercise. FooFoo had to get the net and fish her out.

There were tons of other people on the river, mostly families out for some fun on a beautiful day. All of a sudden Otto's *eye* started pulsing. It was being drawn toward the shore.

"Pull over," he said to FooFoo.

"Oh goody, lunchtime," said FooFoo.

Otto started walking along the riverbank. His *eye* was pulsing wildly. It was practically popping out of his head. This must be what his parents meant

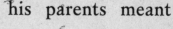

about keeping his *eye* out when they told him he was an undercover spy.

His *eye* jerked to the right. Otto turned his head.

There were two holes drilled into the canyon wall. He walked over to have a closer look. Inside, the holes were filled with *TNT*.

Otto gasped. He looked at the timer. It was set to go off in eight minutes. He remembered the old proverb.

CHAPTER 8

The Old Proverb

Where there are two holes, there might be a million more.

Otto had found his mission.

CHAPTER 9

The Bad Guy

Remember the little girl with the Weewee the Pup tent and the 10,000 sticks of dynamite?

Yes!

The Bad Guy

Turns out she wasn't a girl at all. She was a guy, named Charles William Engelbert III. But he was known as Chinstrap.

This is because once when he was playing with dynamite, his lower jaw and chin fell off his face, and now he had to strap them on every day with a strap that tied on top of his head. He was alone, except for his only friend, a cockroach.

Chinstrap was evil.

"Yes, my little kitty," Chinstrap said, petting his cockroach. "Eight minutes, and it will all be over."

You might ask why Chinstrap called his cockroach "kitty." There doesn't seem to be any good answer to that question.

On second thought, there is one.
Chinstrap was nuts.

CHAPTER 10

No Time for Fish Balls

Otto ran back to the raft.

"Uncle *OrfOrf*, someone is trying to dynamite the canyon. We have to get to the top and find the detonator."

"Well, that's a good plan," said FooFoo. "We'll do it right after lunch."

"Sorry, we'll have lunch to go. We only have eight minutes to do this . . . um, seven minutes," Otto said, looking at his watch.

"How about just an appetizer. I made some nice North Pacific oyster croquettes, and some salt fish balls, nice," said FooFoo.

That hurt.

His aunt made some prize-winning fish balls.

"Uncle *IrfIrf*," he yelled. "How long will it take us to get out of here?" FiFi was great at math.

FiFi, knee-deep in river muck, struggled with a tin can that was stuck to her fishing hook.

She looked around. "Climbing is the quickest way to the top. By my calculations,

it would take us three days to hike up. If
FroFro carried us both, and ran, we could
make it by sunset."

By that time they would all be blown
to smithereens. Otto had to do some . . .

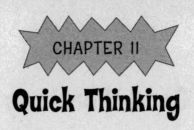

Quick Thinking

Uhmm, thought Otto.

This might take a while, so if all that talk of oysters and fish balls made you hungry, you can take a break now and get a snack.

Wait a minute, come back. He finished thinking.

Good Vibrations

"We've got to get Racecar to come to us!" he said. Otto took out his pocket watch remote control. He spoke into it.

"Ignition On," he said. The remote flashed, *"Out of range."*

He had another idea.

"Uncle FriFri, give me your tuning fork, quick." She always carried one to help her find the note of A-flat when she sang.

"Well, come and get it, boy, and bring a pair of scissors while you're at it." FiFi was completely tangled up in the fishing line.

Otto ran over, snipped the line, and took the tuning fork out of her pocket. He banged it lightly on her head. The vibration of fork on head made a sound that was out of the range of human hearing. It could only be heard by the Giant Cacawewy bird in New Guinea and the *Voice Receptor* in Racecar's ignition.

Then Otto sat down on the ground and pulled one of his shoelaces. A computer screen popped up from the toe of his shoe. The screen showed some lines in the shape of a truck, with the label "Option Nine."

Otto took the end of his shoelace and pressed it to the screen, where it read "Option Two." The lines started to shift.

Then Otto put up his portable collapsible *Radar Tracking and Guiding Device*.

It was in his ring.

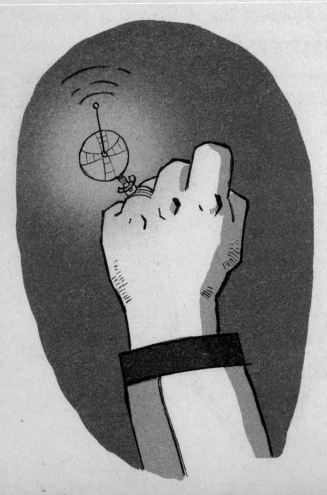

CHAPTER 13

In the Parking Lot

An old man on a walker was in the parking lot with his granddaughter when Racecar was activated. What they saw turned out to be a life-changing experience for both of them.

Years later the little girl became a famous filmmaker and made a movie about their experience.

It was called *The Disappearing Ice-Cream Truck*.

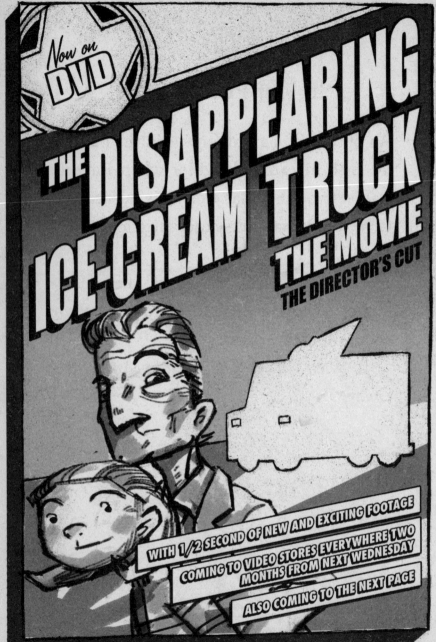

DVD is a palmarome.

THE DISAPPEARING ICE-CREAM TRUCK

SCREENPLAY BY **MARCIA VON BONBON**

SCENE 1

An old man and his granddaughter are waiting for an ice-cream truck to open up. Suddenly the engine turns itself on.

OLD MAN:

What the...?

LITTLE GIRL:

I want vanilla.

The ice-cream truck starts to bubble and heat up.

OLD MAN:

She's gonna blow!

He holds on to his walker and drags the little girl behind a bush for safety.

LITTLE GIRL:

I want vanilla.

The frame of the ice-cream truck turns into a blob of firm jelly.

OLD MAN:

Do you see that?

LITTLE GIRL:

(loudly) I want vanilla!

In seconds the thing that was the ice-cream truck transforms into one of the most unique and coolest-looking cars ever built.

OLD MAN:

Would you look at that there automobile? It's part Ferrari, part Lamborghini, part Jaguar, with a little bit of BMW, Corvette, Porsche, and I don't know what else. Don't that beat all?

LITTLE GIRL:

(very loudly) I want vanilla!!

55

The car honks its horn three times, backs itself smoothly out of the parking spot, and drives itself down the road.

OLD MAN:

Well, now I've seen everything. I feel young again.

He throws away his walker.

LITTLE GIRL:

How about chocolate?

THE END

CHAPTER 14

Back to Our Story

Meanwhile, back at the Weewee the Pup tent, Chinstrap heard footsteps. It was a park ranger. Of all the people Chinstrap hated besides everyone in the world, it was park rangers. When he was a kid, he had gotten kicked out of the Junior Ranger Program in the Grand Canyon for pushing the counselor off the rim and throwing candy wrappers everywhere.

Now he was barred from entering the Grand Canyon. There were pictures of him posted at all the guard gates. He had fooled the guard this time with that nifty little-girl disguise.

The ranger knocked on the tent.

"Are you okay in there, little girl?" asked the ranger.

"Oh yes, Mr. Ranger," said Chinstrap in a high voice.

Chinstrap came skipping out of the tent.

"Where is your mommy or daddy or legal guardian?" asked the ranger.

"Oh, they'll be right back. They went to get me a soda in an official Super-Duper Grand Canyon cup, because I dropped mine and I was crying and throwing a tantrum."

"You look mighty familiar," said the ranger, trying to remember where he had seen this girl before. "Say, have you ever been in the Junior Ranger Program for children 9 to 13 years old?"

"Nope, I'm only 8," said Chinstrap.

"My, you're a very large little girl for

your age," said the ranger.

"You're bad," said Chinstrap. "You shouldn't say I'm too big and fat for my age because that makes fun of me 'cause you're mean and that makes me cry and throw another tantrum."

Chinstrap lay down on the ground, banging his hands and wailing.

"Sorry, sorry," said the ranger. "You're a

very pretty little cupcake of a girl, just
delightful, and I'll be going now." He
quickly left the campsite.

Chinstrap yelled after him, "I'm telling on
you, you stupid meany dumb dumb
stupid!"

When the ranger was out of sight,
Chinstrap rolled on his back and started
laughing.

He took his cockroach out of his dress
pocket. "Isn't it exciting, itty-bitty kitty,"
said Chinstrap, tickling the roach with his

pigtail. "Pretty soon the dynamite is gonna go off and there won't be any more Grand Canyon. The two sides will be all closed together, and it'll be a Grand Flat."

"Are you gonna move mountains?" Chinstrap heard the cockroach say, even though the words were in his own head.

"Yes, my pet," said Chinstrap. "And then people will be afraid of me and make me the president of the world. And you will be the kitty of the world."

The cockroach looked at Chinstrap and pooped.

CHAPTER 15

Really Bad News

Racecar was zooming toward Otto. When the car got closer, the remote control pocket watch started flashing *"In Range."* Otto switched off the *radar* and turned on the video tracking.

He put Racecar in *Unicycle Mode* and navigated him down the steep, jagged canyon wall.

When Racecar made it to the shore, Otto pulled up the *Uni-wheel*, and he and The Aunts got in.

"*Infrared*," said Otto. *The Infrared Windshield* came up.

"*Telescope*," said Otto. Now he had a view of the entire canyon wall.

"Oh no," said Otto. "This is worse than I thought."

Thousands of laser beams were shooting out from one point on the canyon's rim, to holes all along the canyon walls. Each hole was filled with *TNT*.

"The whole canyon is going to blow!" he said.

"That is bad," said FooFoo. "We should go back to the beach."

"No way," said Otto. "If the canyon explodes, the entire state of Arizona could cave in on itself, which could make much of the surrounding states of Utah, New

Mexico, California, Colorado, Nevada, and the country of Mexico also cave in. All of these caving-in states could cause a chain reaction of state caving that would end up destroying all of North America."

"No beach?" asked FooFoo sadly.

"Not today," replied Otto.

"Okay, listen up, everybody. Pay attention, and nobody will get hurt," shouted FiFi.

In emergencies FiFi always liked to be called General and give lots of orders.

"Everyone form a straight line and exit the building quietly. Women and children first."

"Oh, that's us," said FooFoo, pulling off her mustache. "Let's go."

"This isn't a building, General," said Otto. "It's a car. And please put your mustache back on, Uncle *OrfOrf*."

"Good work, Private," said FiFi. "I just

wanted to make sure you were on your toes. Car," she ordered, "all hands on deck, duck and cover, man the sirens!"

"Catapult Hook," said Otto, giving Racecar a command he understood.

A huge catapult hook shot out of Racecar and dug itself into the rim of the canyon.

"Up," said Otto.

Racecar, with the three passengers, began an elevatorlike climb up the catapult rope to the top of the canyon.

The people on the river applauded. They thought the whole thing was a stunt. They couldn't wait to see the next trick.

CHAPTER 16

Three Minutes Left

As soon as they got to the top, Otto turned on Racecar's **Bloodhound Tracking Gear**. It was designed to sniff out explosives, and it didn't take long to find the Weewee the Pup tent.

"I want to see what's going on in that tent," said Otto.

"Wrong," said FiFi. "You are just a small boy, and that could be dangerous. I will decide who goes into the tent. Go ahead, FooFoo."

"Gee," said FooFoo, "I'd love to, but that's a Weewee the Pup tent, and I'm allergic to dogs and all tents that are named after dogs. Who's your second choice?"

"You are," said FiFi.

"There's only three minutes left before this turns into a total canyon catastrophe," said Otto. "I'm the secret agent. I'm going in."

"If it's a secret, why are you telling us?" asked FooFoo.

"I'll be perfectly safe," said Otto, ignoring his aunt. "I'll just pretend I'm a lost kid. If there's a bad guy in there, he'll never suspect anything. *IrfIrf*, watch the car. *OrfOrf*, put the headset on, and I'll talk to you through this microphone." Otto had a mike hidden in his shirt.

CHAPTER 17

A Conversation

Otto was about to enter, but before he could open the canvas, Chinstrap burst through the opening.

"Help!" he screamed, and jumped into Otto's arms.

"Save me, save me," he was crying hysterically.

FooFoo was listening on the head-set. "Someone needs to be saved," she repeated. She was facing away from the tent. She never thought of turning around so she could see what was going on.

"Uh-oh," said FiFi, who was facing the

tent and could see what was going on.

"I'll save you," said Otto.

"Someone is saving someone," said FooFoo.

"That's good," said FiFi.

"What happened to you?" Otto asked the little girl.

"The bad man kidnapped me," said Chinstrap.

"A bad man kidnapped some-one," said FooFoo.

"That's terrible," said FiFi.

"Is he still in there?" asked Otto.

"I don't know," said Chinstrap, holding on to Otto and crying really hard.

Otto couldn't hold Chinstrap anymore. They both fell to the ground.

"You dropped me!" screamed Chinstrap.

"Someone dropped someone else," repeated FooFoo.

"Whoops," said FiFi.

"FroFro, come here," said Otto into the mike.

"Someone named FroFro should go there," said FooFoo.

"That's you," said FiFi.

"Right," said FooFoo.

She ran over to Otto.

"Uncle FroFro, take this little girl to the car, and watch her while I go check out the tent," said Otto.

Otto still had to find the detonator. What he didn't know was that it was in the pocket of Chinstrap's dress.

"You go with my uncles," said Otto to Chinstrap. "They'll take care of you."

"Okay," said Chinstrap, blowing his nose on FroFro's shirt.

Eeuuuu, thought Otto.

*For a little girl, she has **tons o' snot.***

72

a Fairy Tale

FooFoo took Chi... over to Racecar and FiFi.

"Don't worry, wee on..." said FooFoo. "No bad men are going to bo...r you anymore. Here, have this nice homemade candy that I made when I was an aunt, but now I'm an uncle."

"You were an aunt?" asked Chinstrap, munching loudly on the candy.

"I mean, that was a joke," said FooFoo, realizing she shouldn't have said anything about being an aunt. "Oh, what a funny uncle I am. What's your name?" she asked, changing the subject.

"Snow White," said Chinstrap, drooling candy juice.

"What a nice name," said FooFoo. "Isn't

that a nice name, brother FriFiFi, who
"Yeah, great name," more like one
thought that Chinstrap lCinderella.
of the ugly stepsisters
"I can't find the ...nator," came Otto's
voice over FooF... headset.

"That's ok, take your time," answered
FooFoo. We're having lots of fun here
with Snow White."

"Can I sit in the pretty car and make
believe I'm driving?" asked Chinstrap.

"Certainly," said FooFoo.

"Yippee," said Chinstrap, jumping up and
down and clapping his hands. He sat down
behind the wheel.

"Hey, Snow White, isn't that bow on top of
your head kind of tight?" asked FiFi.

FooFoo looked up. "Oh, she's right,
Snow White. You could cut off your circu-
lation that way, and blood would stop
pumping to your brain."

Before Chinstrap could stop her, FiFi leaned over the seat and untied the bow. The wig came off in her hand, and Chinstrap's lower face fell to the floor.

The Uncles Screamed

"Aaaaaaaiiiiiiiiiihhhh
hh!!!!!!!!!!!!!!!!!!!!!!!!!!!!!!!!!!!!!!
!!!!!!!!!!!!!!!!!!!!!!!!!!!!!!!!!!!!!!!"

Running and Screaming

It all happened in an instant.

Otto heard the screams and started running toward Racecar.

Chinstrap started frantically pressing buttons on the steering wheel and dashboard. Lucky for him, he hit the *Rear Cage* switch. The cage went up, the doors locked, and The Uncles were trapped in the back.

The Uncles screamed some more.

Otto ran some more.

Chinstrap turned on the engine and streaked out of the place.

CHAPTER 21

What Happened Next

Next Otto yelled, "Come back!"

Next nobody did.

Next Otto almost said a bad word.

Then he remembered

CHAPTER 22

Memory Number One

the *Microscopic Magnet* implanted in his earlobe.

CHAPTER 23

Magnetic Force

Otto wrapped his arms around a tree and squeezed his ear. This sent a powerful charge to a magnetic strip that ran through Racecar's *Mission Shell*. Chinstrap had his foot on the gas pedal, but Racecar was being pulled backward toward Otto's ear.

The Aunts were struggling to pull the cage off.

Racecar was now about six feet away from Otto's ear. Otto couldn't hold on to the tree anymore. The magnetic force pulled Otto off his feet, and

80

he flew the rest of the way, ear first. Otto's face was now pressed against the side of the car.

Once the magnets were touching, there was nothing to stop Racecar from going forward. Chinstrap still had his foot on the gas, and they lurched away, speeding toward the canyon exit.

CHAPTER 24

A Way In

Otto hung on to Racecar, the magnetic force running through his entire body. With all his strength, he climbed the car, pulling himself up one limb at a time.

An arm, a leg, an arm, a leg. He ran out of limbs.

He thought of using the same ones again. An arm, a leg, an arm, a leg. That turned out to be a good idea.

Now he was on top.

"Roof Panel!" he screamed.

"Got it," said FooFoo. She pressed a button.

The panel opened, and Chinstrap saw Otto looking down at him from the top of the car.

"Hi," said Otto.

"Hi," said Chinstrap.

Otto squeezed twice, deactivating the magnet. He fell into the passenger seat, right next to Chinstrap.

40 Seconds Left

Chinstrap was steering with one hand and holding his chin with the other. The detonator was sitting right next to him on the seat.

"There it is," said Otto. "I've been looking all over for that thing."

Otto carefully put his hand on the detonator. Chinstrap dropped his chin and put his hand on top of Otto's. Otto put his other hand on top of Chinstrap's.

Chinstrap took his other hand off the steering wheel and put it on top of Otto's.

There was no one driving the car. Otto grabbed the steering wheel with his foot.

"Get your hands off the detonator," he said to Chinstrap.

It's pretty hard to talk without a lower jaw. "Ehh uie oue. Ehh ou ouui eoaaaoee," said Chinstrap.

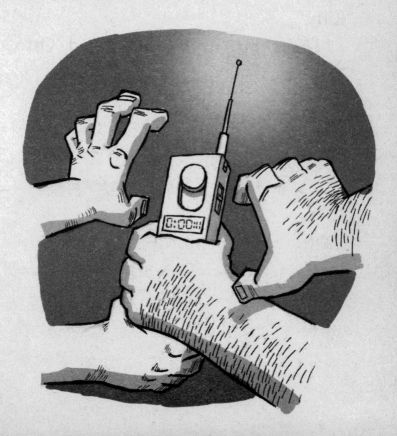

What he meant was, "No, it's mine. Get your own detonator."

Otto looked at the clock on the detonator. There were only 40 seconds left before everything was set to blow up.

Just then Chinstrap's pet cockroach crawled out of Chinstrap's dress and started creeping down his arm.

"Iiyy," said Chinstrap, which meant "Kitty."

"That's no 'iiyy'!!!" screamed Otto. "That's a

CHAPTER 27

A Bug Jumps, a Car Falls

In the longest recorded cockroach leap in history, the bug jumped out of the open roof panel.

Chinstrap immediately took his hands off the detonator.

He yelled, "Iiyy, uoh aaah!" which meant "Kitty, come back," and he started climbing out of the panel after it.

You'd think this was a good thing, and it was. There was just one problem. When he saw the roach, Otto took his hands off the detonator too. He also took his foot off the steering wheel. Without anyone driving, Racecar went right off the cliff. They were all falling down the huge drop into the Grand Canyon.

CHAPTER 28

A Man, a Tree, and Colored Wires

The Grand Canyon is more than a mile deep. It takes about 30 seconds to fall that far. Thirty seconds is not a very long time, but sometimes it's all you've got.

The first thing Otto did was wish he had put a propeller on Racecar so he could fly. That took up 3 seconds and was a waste of time. Then he joined The Aunts in an ear-piercing scream. That took 5 more seconds and was a waste of time too. Then Otto decided to not waste any more time. That took 2 seconds, but it was worth it.

He smashed his hand down on the *Voice Command* button.

"Cage Down,"
he said.

The cage went down, and The Aunts were free.

"The detonator is set to go off in 14 seconds. We have 19 seconds left before we crash . . . ooo, now we have 18."

Meanwhile, Chinstrap had found his "kitty," and was trying to get back into the car through the panel.

FiFi yelled, **"Panel Close."** But Chinstrap's leg was already halfway through it, and the panel couldn't close. She grabbed his foot and tried to push him back out.

Otto was looking for the timer wire. He had never dismantled a detonator before. He very, very carefully took off the cover.

FiFi was struggling with Chinstrap's foot. She bit his ankle. He kicked her in the face. FiFi's tooth fell out. Luckily, it was a false tooth. She put it back in.

Otto studied the inside of the device. There were dozens of different colored wires, all looping around and going into the timer. He didn't know which one to pull out.

Chinstrap reached an arm into the car. His fingers were just an inch away from grabbing the detonator.

"I have an idea," said FooFoo excitedly.

"That's swell," said FiFi, wrestling Chinstrap's arm. "WHAT IS IT?"

"CLAW!" she shouted.

A helmet with a *Virtual Visor* dropped down from Racecar's roof. FiFi got into position and clipped it over her head. An *Electronic Sleeve* came out of the glove compartment, and FiFi slipped her hand into it. Now FiFi could see and move as though she was the *CLAW*.

"Everybody keep quiet!" said Otto to no one. The pressure was intense. Otto knew that there was only one right wire to pull. "There are only 3 seconds left," he said.

FiFi saw Chinstrap through the visor. She moved her arm over and opened her hand. The **CLAW** opened up. Then she closed her hand, and the **CLAW** closed around Chinstrap.

"Got him," she said.

"Two seconds," said Otto. He was going

to have to do something now!

"I'm 99 percent sure I should pull this green one," he said.

"No, Ottie, don't. I'm 99½ percent sure it's the *violet* one," said FooFoo. "I *love it*. It's the prettiest."

FiFi picked Chinstrap up in the **CLAW** and extended her hand way out. Chinstrap was hanging above the Grand Canyon, kicking and screaming.

Otto wanted to pull the green wire, but he still had a tiny doubt. "That 1 percent is killing me," he said.

"Wait!" said FooFoo. "I changed my mind. Pull the yellow one. Yellow's my favorite color."

FiFi saw a high tree on the side of the canyon. She quickly moved Chinstrap over to it.

There was 1 second left. "Okay, I'm gonna do it," said Otto, wiping the sweat

95

off his hands.

"Hold everything!" said FooFoo. "I forgot, yellow isn't my favorite color anymore. I hate yellow. Pull the red one."

"A quarter of a second," said Otto. "This is it."

"No. Stop," screamed FooFoo. "Pull the blue one! I know it's the blue one because I once had a blue dress."

FiFi opened her hand, and the CLAW dropped Chinstrap on the highest branch of the tree.

There was $1/16$ of a second left.

Otto's fingers were about to close on the green wire.

"Bull's-eye," said FiFi, and then she jerked her arm back.

Her elbow hit Otto's hand. His fingers picked up the orange wire.

"That's it!" said Otto.

FooFoo screamed, "Not the orange one!"

Otto pulled the orange wire. He held his breath for a whole page.

Breath Holding

This is the page where Otto held his breath.

CHAPTER 30

Otto Breathes

The clock stopped ticking.

Nothing blew up.

Otto let out his breath. Then he remembered something.

CHAPTER 31

Memory Number Two

They were still falling.

CHAPTER 32

Auto Gymnastics

What with all the breath holding and remembering, they had wasted 3 whole seconds. There were only 2 seconds left till Racecar crashed at full force onto the bottom of the Grand Canyon.

Otto yelled, *"Spring!"*

"Who cares what season it is," said FiFi.

Racecar's wheels rolled up, and a giant spring came out.

"Oh, that spring," said FiFi.

Racecar hit the canyon floor. He immediately sprang up again, twice as far. They bounced again and again, each time gaining height, like on a

mega-powerful trampoline.

Otto was so happy they weren't going to crash that he steered Racecar into some trick moves. He did a front flip, a double back flip, and a front-wheel stand into a back-wheel spring.

A huge crowd of people were watching the show from the top of the canyon. They were having a great time. Not one of them was aware of the catastrophic canyon catastrophe that had almost blown them all to smithereens.

CHAPTER 33

It's Not Over Yet

Otto and The Aunts couldn't stick around for the applause. They had to get out of there before people found out who they really were. They also had to let someone know about the dynamite still in the canyon walls.

Their last bounce landed them on a deserted part of the canyon rim.

"Let's roll," said FiFi.

"It's too late," said Otto. A line of cars was streaming down the road toward them. "Take off your disguises, quick," he yelled to The Uncles.

Then he said, *"Straw warts,"* which was his favorite palindrome command. The Mission frame heated into a jelly. A funnel opened up in the trunk, and the jelly was sucked into it. There it turned liquid and was stored in an emptied-out tuna can. Racecar was now his old self again.

He looked at his aunts. They were standing in the middle of the road in their underwear.

"Where are your dresses?" asked Otto.

"Put on your dresses!"

"We forgot to bring them," said FooFoo.

"Whoops," said Otto.

CHAPTER 34

Here Comes the Ranger

A ranger truck and six cars screeched to a halt in front of them.

It was time for some more quick thinking.

"Start crying," said Otto to The Aunts.

You can't get much quicker than that.

10-4

FooFoo and FiFi were wailing.

The ranger jumped out of his car. He was the same ranger who had talked to Chinstrap at the Weewee the Pup tent earlier. "Are you all right, ladies?"

"No, they're upset and very chilly," said Otto. "An ugly man came and took their clothes," he lied.

"Why?" asked the ranger.

"Because, uhm, they were his size, I guess. He said something about his chin and a strap and blowing up the Grand Canyon. It was very scary."

"Very scary," wailed The Aunts.

"I knew that Weewee the Pup tent girl looked familiar," said the ranger, slapping himself on the head.

He took out his car radio and called in to headquarters.

"10–4, 10–4," said the ranger.

"Go ahead," said the voice from headquarters.

"6–80, 3–40, 2–70," said the ranger.

"Nice numbers," said the voice. "What do you want?"

"Oh right," said the ranger. "Send someone down to check the canyon for explosives, and look around for an ugly man with no chin."

"That would be a 6–80, 3–40, 2–70," said the voice.

"10–4," said the ranger.

"Say, you look familiar too," said the ranger to Otto. "And so does this car." He was running his hands over Racecar.

Otto swallowed hard. Their secret agent days might be over with only one mission accomplished.

"I've got it," said the ranger. "You're that kid racecar driver, and this is your car!"

"Yes sir, Otto Pillip is my name," said Otto, feeling relieved. "Nice to meet you."

"Nice to meet you, too," said the ranger, shaking Otto's hand like it was a water pump. "I used to be a big fan. Not

anymore. There's this other kid with a cooler car who's a lot better than you. He was here doing some swell tricks a few minutes ago. Did ya see him?"

"Dinnertime," yelled FooFoo. "Let's beat it."

To the surprise of everyone, The Aunts jumped into the car in their underwear. Otto drove away laughing his head off.

CHAPTER 36

Finders Keepers

The rangers found the dynamite. But although they looked for many days, they never did find Chinstrap. That's because the Giant Cacawewy bird found him first.

CHAPTER 37

Caca Whoey?

The Giant Cacawewy bird was standing around on one leg, a few continents away in New Guinea, when Otto hit FiFi's head with the tuning fork. That was waaay back in Chapter 12. No kidding, look it up.

The Cacawewy had just broken up with her boyfriend and was feeling kind of lonely and blue. When she heard the high-pitched vibrations, she got goose bumps on her wing feathers and flew off in search of love.

Being a fast flyer, the Giant Cacawewy arrived at the Grand Canyon about half an hour later.

Chinstrap was clinging to a branch at the top of a tree. The cockroach was on his head. He was calling for help, but with half a mouth the word *help* sounded more like a squawky "heh, heehhh, hehhhhh."

Following the sounds, the Giant Caca-wewy swooped down on the tree and saw Chinstrap. Naturally, she mistook him for another bird.

It was love at first sight. She was pretty hungry, so first she ate the cockroach. Then she picked Chinstrap up in her beak and flew off with him to a nest somewhere far, far away.

eye

Eee YiiiY Eee • Super Agents

Do you like it? We know how much you love to sing. All the Eboys are very musically talented. We tuned all six strings to the note G, because that's your note. Did you know there are many other notes in the musical scale? We know two of them. Mom's is called C and Dad's is called E. They're quite nice. You might want to learn them someday.

Oh, one more thing. Please put on your dolphin water wings and learn to swim. This is important because secret agents often get thrown into the deep end of the pool.

We love you even more than we did on the other side of this letter.

Mom and Dad

P.S. Sorry, but for your own safety, this letter is now going to crumble to dust.

a barn. It was called "The Enormous Roadside Diner in a Barn."

The parking lot was inside. People recognized Racecar, Otto gave a ton of autographs, and all the kids took turns sitting in the car.

FooFoo really needed to cook. If she went too many hours without cooking, she would come down with a fever. They let her take over the kitchen, and because much of Arizona is a desert, she made 32 different cactus-based dishes including French-fried cactus, cactus in oyster sauce, and raw cactus with wasabi.

FiFi, who couldn't care less that they were in Arizona, sang the song "Oklahoma" in the note of A-flat while leading the customers in a tap-dancing line dance.

"Okay, everybody, I have a song," said Otto.

But he didn't. He opened his mouth and nothing came out.

"Guess I'm tired," said Otto, a little embarrassed. "Maybe next time."

"That's all right, I've got another one," said FiFi. She started singing "Georgia."

CHAPTER 39

A Delivery

It was pretty late when the last customer left the diner. The owner asked Otto and The Aunts if they wanted to stay in his extra room for the night. The Aunts, who both thought the owner was cute, said yes. Otto said sure, if he could sleep with Racecar. The Aunts agreed, and Otto and Racecar were left alone in the diner.

Otto lay down on Racecar's hood.

"You did great today," Otto said to Racecar.

"You did too," Otto said to himself.

Otto was happy, but a little bit sad, too.

"I wish my parents could be here, don't you?" he said to Racecar.

"I sure do," Otto answered himself.

He took out his pocket watch and

opened the secret compartment that contained his parents' letter.

"Let's read it again," said Otto.

The letter was blank because it was written in invisible ink, but Otto remembered every word.

"Do you think it would be all right if you called me *Jake* just one time?" whispered Otto. He loved his real name. "Nobody's here."

"Jake," Otto whispered to himself.

Just then Otto heard a shuffling on the gravel outside the door to the diner. Then he heard a loud knocking. It was 3:00 in the morning. Kind of late for customers. Otto looked out the window. It was very dark outside, and spooky. He decided not to answer the door. Then there was more loud knocking, and a voice.

"Delivery," said the voice.

"The diner is closed," said Otto. "The owner isn't here."

"This is a delivery for *Toot Lippil*," said the voice.

Otto knew his name when he heard it. "Hey, that's me," he said. "Just a minute."

Otto went to the door and opened it a little bit. He couldn't see anybody. He opened it all the way. There was nobody there. There was a box, though. A pretty big one. There was an envelope taped to it, addressed to *Toot Lippil*.

Otto took in the box and locked the door. He was very excited. He tore off the envelope and opened it up. There was a letter inside. He read it out loud.

Dear Jake, Our Son Whom We Love
So Much,

It's your parents, Hogarth and
Eleanor Eboy. Wonderful job today.
You saved thousands of people. Maybe
millions.

That spring invention was brilliant,
not to mention the magnetic ear. Wish
we had one of those.

If you feel a little sad after your
mission, you should know that's okay.
It's very lonely to keep secrets. Remember,
we are always with you, even though we're
not.

Boy, does that sound dumb.

This is a good time to look in the box.
Then turn this paper over.

CHAPTER 40

In the Box

Otto tore open the box. He gasped when he saw what was inside. It was an electric guitar. The most beautiful electric guitar he'd ever seen. And an amplifier. He didn't realize until that moment that he wanted an electric guitar more than anything in the world, besides seeing his parents.

He turned the letter over.

CHAPTER 38

Dinner and Dancing

Otto bought his aunts some Annie Oakley cowgirl outfits at a souvenir shop. Otto was just too happy to drive all the way home. He had to stop somewhere to do the twist.

They were all starving anyway, so they drove into an enormous roadside diner in

And it did.

Otto didn't even care. He was so happy. He did a little twist. Then he picked up the guitar and plugged it into the amp. He strummed the strings. Boy, did they sound good. Now he had a song. No one else was there, so he sang to Racecar.

Nate Bit a Tibetan
(In the note of G, with guitar)

To - day is my fa - vor - ite day - o

Be - sides yes - ter - day and the day

be - fore that - o To - mor - row is good

too - o And the day af - ter that

is al - so ex - cell - ent - o

An - oth - er good day is ev - er - y

Thurs - day - o

And all days that have 4:00 in them -

o - o

do de o do do de - o do do de o

CHAPTER 41

The End.

CHAPTER 42

Really The End.